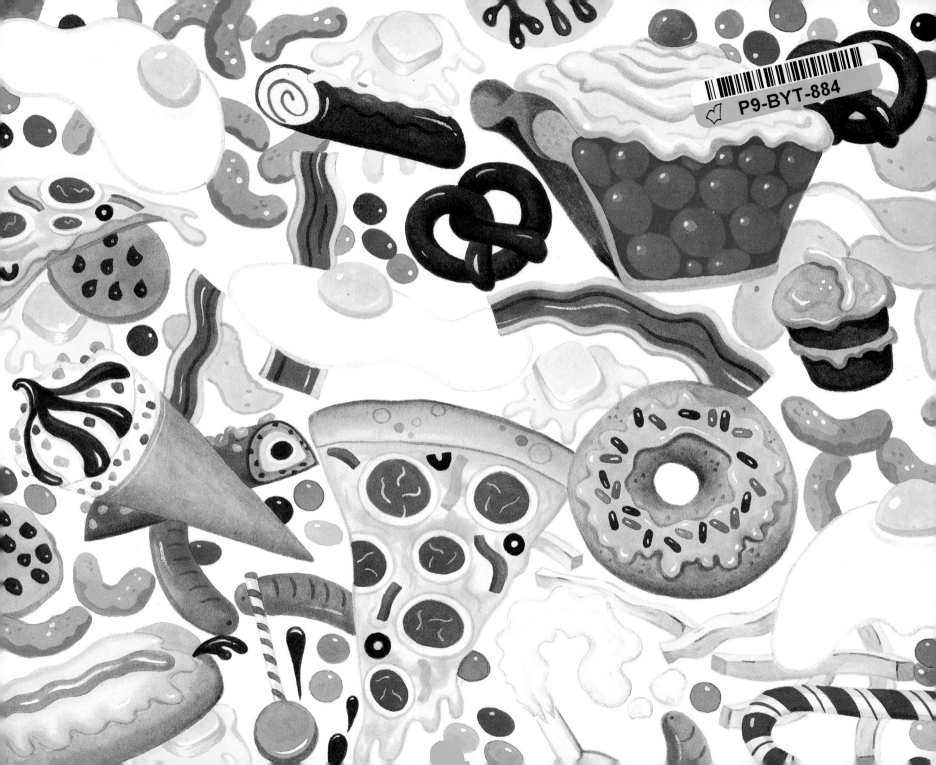

P9-BYT-884

For Julia Child, who once said to me,
"Eat, drink, and be merry, for tomorrow we diet."
—*D.D.*

For Teddy
—*C.S.*

Dom DeLuise's

Hansel & Gretel

illustrated by

Christopher Santoro

Simon & Schuster Books for Young Readers

ONCE UPON A TIME, there lived a poor family who worked very hard to keep themselves in food and clothing. They lived from hand to mouth, and, let's face it, that's a very short distance.

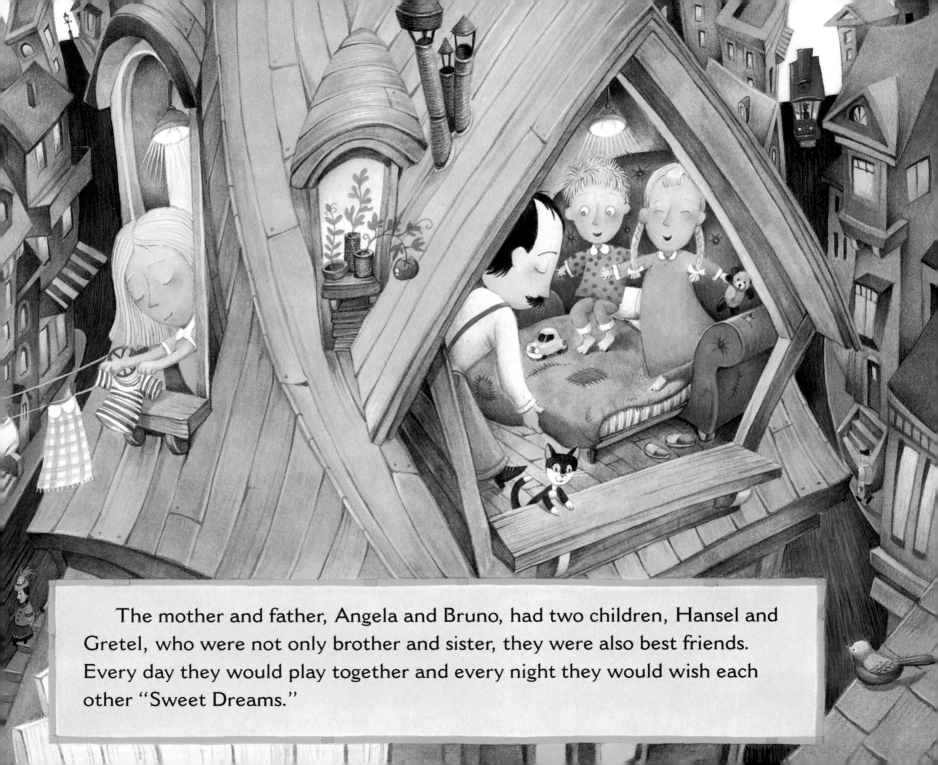

The mother and father, Angela and Bruno, had two children, Hansel and Gretel, who were not only brother and sister, they were also best friends. Every day they would play together and every night they would wish each other "Sweet Dreams."

Angela wanted Hansel and Gretel to grow up strong and healthy. She fed them

fresh vegetables, fresh fruits, and beans. . . . non-fat dairy products, grains, fish,

Ah, but we'll hear from the beans later.

Every morning they ate healthy, delicious hot oatmeal with skim milk, and they shared some fresh fruit. For lunch they ate vegetables and fat-free chicken soup.

After lunch the children would ask for apple pie à la mode with chocolate sauce.

"Oh my, no," said their mother. "Have some healthy

an [apple] or a [banana] for dessert."

"Ah," said Hansel and Gretel.

"We just want a sugar fix!" Their mother said . . .

"I don't think so"

Then one day their mother became very ill, and soon after, she died. Their father was very sad. Hansel and Gretel missed their mother so much, they would cry themselves to sleep.

Now, next door there lived the Widow Brown, who wanted to marry their father in the worst way. Why, she brought him chicken soup every single day. If you're looking for a new husband, chicken soup is a must. Bruno really liked the Widow Brown's chicken soup, so they were soon married.

Unfortunately, the Widow Brown was <u>not</u> very fond of children. Oh, dear!

One evening, while Hansel and Gretel were asleep, a beautiful butterfly landed on Gretel's nose and woke her up. Gretel heard the Widow Brown talking to her father.

"THERE'S NOT ENOUGH MONEY AND FOOD IN THIS HOUSE FOR ALL OF US. LET'S TAKE THE CHILDREN FOR A PICNIC AND **LEAVE THEM IN THE WOODS.** ANOTHER FAMILY WILL FIND THEM, TAKE THEM HOME, AND CARE FOR THEM. THE CHILDREN WILL BE MUCH HAPPIER AND SO WILL WE."

"No, no," said Bruno. "I love my children. I couldn't. I just couldn't."

Gretel was Very Upset to say the least. What to do? What to do?

The very next night both Hansel and Gretel heard the Widow Brown talking.

"TAKE THEM TO THE WOODS, I TELL YOU! MAKE SOME EXCUSE AND LEAVE THEM THERE. SOMEONE WILL FIND AND CARE FOR THEM. NOT TO WORRY"

Bruno said nothing.

WORRY!

But Hansel and Gretel started to—guess what?
Wouldn't you? I would!

"We need a plan," said Gretel. Hansel agreed.

Remember the beans from before? Well, early
the next morning Hansel and Gretel filled their pockets
with dry beans to drop along the path. Those beans would help them find
their way home. "Children, we are going on a picnic in the woods," said
the Widow Brown. They started walking. Hansel and Gretel lagged
behind dropping beans along the way.

Soon they were deep in the woods. "Let's have our picnic here," said the Widow Brown. "You children rest. Your father and I will get some firewood." And they left. Hansel and Gretel caught each other's eye. They were alone.

ALONE! Oh my!

It got so quiet they could hear the crickets chirping and the leaves rustling. Why, they could even hear a dewdrop drop!

"Don't worry," said Gretel. "We've got a plan. We'll find our way back. We'll just follow our trail of beans." They started home, but most of the beans had been eaten by squirrels, rabbits, and who knows what else! "Our bean trail has been eaten! Oh, what to do? What to do?" cried Hansel. They both sat down and had a good cry . . . that is, if a cry can be good.

"Wait, Hansel," said Gretel. "I smell cookies baking."

"It's coming from over here!" cried Hansel.

They climbed a small hill and came to a fence that was made of

gum drops

lollipops

giant chocolate
covered pretzel
gate

lady fingers

glazed
donuts

←more donuts↑

"This ladyfinger fence is absolutely delicious!"

The gingerbread house was full of junk food. It had a cholesterol count of 888, which is high, even for a house.

The children were so hungry. They started to eat.

"Yum! Have some chocolate windowsill."

Suddenly

the cupcake doorknob turned, the door flew open, and there stood Glut Annie Stout, a woman as wide as she was tall.

"Who's eating my house?" she called.

"Oh, we're lost," said Gretel.

"Lost?" asked Glut Annie. "Don't worry; I'll take good care of you. Come in. I'm making some sweet apple and blueberry pies. Come in!"

Glut Annie gave them strawberry malteds, apple pie à la mode with chocolate sauce, banana cream pie, and a big piece of chocolate, not five-, not six-, but seven-layer cake. Well, the children ate and ate. They were very tired, so they said their prayers, wished each other "Sweet Dreams," put their heads on marshmallow pillows, and fell fast asleep.

Early the next day the butterfly gently woke the children.

"Good morning," said Hansel and Gretel. Glut Annie Stout served them a very big breakfast of eggs Benedict, bacon, ham, sausage, pancakes, and French toast, all smothered in butter and maple syrup. A calorie counter she wasn't. Hansel and Gretel couldn't finish their food. Glut Annie, however, tasted everything twice.

After breakfast, the children said good-bye and started to leave, but the door was locked. "And just where do you good-for-nothings think you're going?" asked Glut Annie.

"Home, we want to go home," said the children.

"Home? Ha, Ha. Never! You'll live here and help me make puddings, cakes, and pies."

The children trembled. It was clear that Miss Glut Annie Stout was (a) completely unaware of how unhealthy all that fat and sugar is! and (b) not very nice . . . not very nice, indeed! So the children worked as hard as they could helping Glut Annie while she cooked and cooked . . . and cooked.

Later that night the children gathered some fireflies from the open window and had a family meeting under the blanket. What to do? What to do? Glut Annie was so disagreeable, so mean and so cruel. The children made a plan— a plan to run away!

run away!

The next day the children licked a hole in one of the lollipop windows. Gretel boosted Hansel up to unlock the latch. They climbed out, jumped down, and started to run. But Glut Annie Stout was waiting and swooped Hansel and Gretel up in a sticky net made of cotton candy, which clung to their arms, legs, and hair. Glut Annie washed them off in the pond and brought them back into the house. She put Hansel in the kitchen pantry. "That ought to keep you," she said as she locked the gate. She put the key in her apron pocket and said to Gretel, "You won't run away again. You won't leave your brother here, locked up. Now get back to work!" Oh, she was so-o-o-o mean!!

What to do? What to do?

Gretel worked and pondered. She needed another plan.
"Oh, the key!" thought Gretel. "The key is the key!" Days
went by. Unhappy days. Nights went by. Unhappy nights.
Gretel helped the wretched woman cook, and thought
about ways to get that key. Every day Glut Annie sat
down to a fat-filled feast. And every night Gretel had all
those dishes, pots, and pans to clean. Glut Annie
baked and baked . . . and baked, using lots of cream
and butter and eggs, oh my! Then one day came
the straw that broke the camel's back—Glut
Annie burped so loud it stopped the clock,
and she didn't even say, "Excuse me!"

Well, Gretel knew it was time to set her plan in motion. So the very next day she took all the sugar and hid it in a picture of the Good Ship Lollipop—almost sinking it.

Later, when Glut Annie Stout was ready to make her cakes and pies, she shouted, "Sugar! There's no more sugar." She took the key and unlocked the gate. Gretel's plan was working! As Glut Annie entered the pantry, Gretel signaled Hansel to step to one side.

She picked up the broom, swung it wa-a-a-ay back, and with all her might let Glut Annie have it right on her rump roast.

Oh, what a loud thump she made. Hansel ran out. Gretel slammed the gate shut. "Why, you little—" Glut Annie snarled. Oh! But the key was inside. What to do? What to do?

Just then, as if by magic, the butterfly picked up the key from the floor of the pantry and flew to Gretel, who took it and locked the gate just in time. Hansel and Gretel hugged and kissed each other.

Using the key, Gretel opened the front door, and they ran through the woods to a recently installed public telephone. Thank goodness Alexander Graham Bell lived in the neighborhood. They called 911.

The police soon came and took Glut Annie Stout into custody.
She was charged with

Now, months before, Bruno, realizing he had made a mistake, had sent the Widow Brown packing. She was never heard from again. Good riddance! So when the police told Bruno that Hansel and Gretel had been found and were safe, he cried, "My dream has come true!" And oh, how happy he was to see Hansel and Gretel, his children that he loved so much.

"I'll never let you out of my sight again!" he said. "I'll always be your loving father."

This was music to the children's ears. "Oh, thank you, Father, thank you! We love you so. We are so glad to be home!" said Hansel and Gretel.

"This calls for a celebration," said Bruno. "Let's have apple pie à la mode with chocolate sauce."

The children turned green at the thought. "No thanks, Dad, just a plain banana would be fine."

Just then the beautiful butterfly appeared. "She's our guardian angel," said Hansel and Gretel.

"Oh," said Bruno, "I thought it was a butterfly." The children laughed as they all had some fat-free chicken soup.

Their loving father opened a very successful health food store called "Bruno's Golden Dream." He took excellent care of his children for many years, and every night they all wished each other not *sweet,* but *golden* dreams (fewer calories). They were a family again. A loving, fat-free, healthy family who lived happily ever after. The end.

Dear Parents,

Young children should never cook by themselves. However, you might enjoy helping them prepare these healthy treats.

Golden Dreams Fat-Free Chicken Soup

FOR WHAT AILS YOU!

SERVES 8

INGREDIENTS:

About 3 quarts water
1 small chicken, about 2 1/2 pounds
1 onion, diced
2 stalks celery, diced
4 tablespoons parsley, minced
2 carrots, diced
2 small tomatoes, diced
1/2 cup of alphabet pasta or pastina
salt, to taste
pepper, to taste

PREPARATION:

Remove skin, fat, and wings from chicken. Put chicken in a large pot and cover with water. Bring to a boil, cover, and cook over medium heat for about one hour. Remove and discard bones, and set chicken meat aside. Skim fat from pot.
Place all vegetables in the pot, cover, and cook another hour.
Add chicken meat and pasta, and cook ten minutes more.
Add salt and pepper to taste.
Serve with bread and salad. Add grated nonfat cheese, if you'd like.

AND A SPOON! DON'T FORGET THE SPOON!

Sugarless Apple Pie

SERVES 6

INGREDIENTS:

3 medium apples, peeled, cored, and sliced
cinnamon
1 tablespoon raisins
1 tablespoon nuts
1/2 cup Grapenuts cereal
1 cup apple juice

PREPARATION:

Preheat oven to 350°.
Place sliced apples in an 8-inch pie dish. Sprinkle cinnamon, raisins, and nuts over apples. Top with Grapenuts. Moisten Grapenuts with apple juice and bake 1 1/2 hours. Serve with low-fat ice cream, nonfat frozen yogurt, or whatever tickles your fancy.

ENJOY!

SIMON & SCHUSTER BOOKS FOR YOUNG READERS
An imprint of Simon & Schuster Children's Publishing Division
1230 Avenue of the Americas, New York, New York 10020

Book design by Anahid Hamparian
The text for this book is set in 15-point Cantoria
The illustrations are rendered in watercolor
Printed and bound in the United States of America
First Edition
10 9 8 7 6 5 4 3 2 1
Library of Congress Cataloging-in-Publication Data
DeLuise, Dom.
Hansel & Gretel / written by Dom DeLuise ; illustrated by Christopher Santoro.
p.   cm.
Summary: An updated, health-conscious version of the Grimm fairy tale in which a brother and sister must outwit a gluttonous
old woman in order to find their way home. Includes recipes for fat-free chicken soup and sugarless apple pie.
ISBN 0-689-81202-7
[1. Fairy tales. 2. Folklore—Germany.] I. Santoro, Christopher, ill.
II. Title.
PZ8.D3755Han 1997
[398.2]—dc20 96-35047